for Charlotte and Antoine

American edition published in 2016 by Andersen Press USA,
an imprint of Andersen Press Ltd.
www.andersenpressusa.com

First published in Great Britain in 2001 by Andersen Press Ltd.,
20 Vauxhall Bridge Road, London SW1V 2SA.

Distributed in the United States and Canada by
Lerner Publishing Group, Inc.
241 First Avenue North
Minneapolis, MN 55401 USA
For reading levels and more information, look up this title at www.lernerbooks.com.

Color separated in Switzerland by Photolitho AG, Zürich.
Printed and bound in Malaysia by Tien Wah Press.

Library of Congress Cataloging-in-Publication Data Available.
ISBN: 978-1-5124-0569-9
eBook ISBN: 978-1-5124-0570-5
1-TWP-7/1/15

ELMER
and GRANDPA ELDO

David McKee

Elmer, the patchwork elephant, was picking fruit.
"Picking fruit, Elmer?" asked a monkey.
"I'm going to see Grandpa Eldo and this is his favorite,"
said Elmer.
"Golden Grandpa Eldo?" asked Monkey. "That's nice."

Grandpa Eldo was pleased to see Elmer.
"What a lovely surprise," he said. "What's that
balanced on your head?"

"Your favorite fruit," said Elmer.
"Fancy you remembering that," said Eldo.
"I remember lots of things," said Elmer.

"What else do you remember?" asked Eldo.
"The walks we used to go on," said Elmer.
"Walks? Where did we go?" Eldo asked.
"Don't you remember?" said Elmer. "I'll
show you. Come on."

"We used to come this way, past the rocks," said Elmer.
"Here I used to hide, then jump out and shout . . ."
Elmer turned around, but Eldo wasn't there.
"Grandpa? Grandpa Eldo, where are you?" he called.

Eldo suddenly jumped out in front of Elmer.
"BOO!" he shouted.
"Oh, Grandpa!" Elmer laughed. "I was supposed to do that. Come on, now we go down to the stream."

At the stream Elmer said,
"Don't you remember anything? We used
to play stepping stones."
"Show me," said Eldo.

There were already some rocks in the water.
Elmer added more to fill in the spaces.
"Now walk across," he said. "Be careful, there's
usually a wobbly one."

Suddenly there was a huge
SPLASH! Elmer had fallen in.
"You were right. You've a good
memory," Eldo chuckled.
Elmer laughed. "Lucky it's not deep."
"Now where?" asked Eldo.
"You still don't remember?" asked Elmer. "To the lake,
of course."

"We used to play Ducks and Drakes," said Elmer. He picked up a flat stone and sent it skipping across the water. "Seven splashes," he said.

"Let me try," said Eldo.

"You need a nice flat stone," said Elmer, but Eldo had already thrown. "1, 2, 3, 4, 5, 6, 7, 8, 9," they counted together.

When they set off again, Elmer started to sing. Eldo joined in, then the birds joined in too.

"When we're marching on our way,
    bumpity bump, bumpity bump.
    We like to laugh and play,
    bumpity bump, bumpity bump.
And when we can't think what to do
We simply hide and then shout, 'BOOOOO!'
When we're marching on our way,
    bumpity bump, bumpity bump!"

When they shouted, "BOO!" the birds flew
    around, squawking with
        laughter.

It started to rain and they
dashed into a cave for shelter.
"Surely you remember the stories you used to
tell me?" Elmer asked.
Eldo frowned."What were they?" he asked.
"*Red Riding Hood*, *Jack and the Beanstalk*,
Cinderella, *Three Little Pigs* . . . Mmmm . . .
Billygoats Gruff . . . Aaaah . . . *Sleeping
Beauty* . . ." Elmer hesitated.
"*Hansel and Gretel*, *Tom Thumb*, *Goldilocks* . . ." Eldo
continued.
"You cheat, you do remember!" said Elmer.

Eldo laughed and, now that the rain had
stopped, ran off. Elmer chased him all the way
back to Eldo's place, shouting, "You tricked me. You
remembered everything. I'll get you, Grandpa Eldo."

After they had their breath back, and stopped laughing, and finished the fruit that Elmer brought, it was time to go home.

"It's been fun, Grandpa," said Elmer. "You really remembered everything, didn't you?"

"Yes," chuckled Eldo, "and I was so happy that you did, too. But best of all, you remembered to visit me."

Elmer smiled. "Bye, Grandpa," he said. "See you soon."